Birthday Rules

By Laurie Friedman

Illustrated by Teresa Murfin

Carolrhoda Books / Minneapolis

For my mom and dad,
with all my love
—L.B.F.

For Harry
—T.M.

E
Friedman,
Laurie

Text copyright © 2015 by Laurie B. Friedman
Illustrations copyright © 2015 by Teresa Murfin

Carolrhoda Books
A division of Lerner Publishing Group, Inc.
241 First Avenue North
Minneapolis, MN 55401 USA

For reading levels and more information, look up this title at www.lernerbooks.com.

Main body text set in Gomorrah Regular.
Typeface provided by Chank.

Library of Congress Cataloging-in-Publication Data

Friedman, Laurie B., 1964–
        Birthday rules / by Laurie Friedman ; illustrated by Teresa Murfin.
            pages   cm
        Summary: Percy Isaac Gifford shares birthday advice, from circling the day on the calendar
to making wishes when blowing out birthday cake candles, reminding the reader that "growing is good."
        ISBN 978-0-7613-6071-1 (lib. bdg. : alk. paper)
        ISBN 978-1-4677-6177-2 (eBook)
        [1. Stories in rhyme. 2. Birthdays—Fiction. 3. Growth—Fiction.] I. Murfin, Teresa, illustrator. II. Title.
PZ8.3.F9116Bk 2015
[E]—dc23   2014011651

Manufactured in the United States of America
1 - DP - 12/31/14

I'm Percy Isaac Gifford, and I'm the **birthday boy**.

Today's a celebration that
makes me jump for joy!

And here's a little secret.
I'm a **birthday pro.**
When it comes to festivities,
There's **nothing** I don't know.

I make the most of my birthday.
I promise you can too.
Just follow these simple rules.
That's all you have to do.

The first thing you should know:
This day comes just once a year.
So enjoy every moment!
It's filled with birthday cheer.

Give me an **H**. Give me an **A**.
Give me a **P-P-Y**.

Then add the word *birthday*.
That's the birthday cry!

RULE #2:
HAPPY TIMES CALL
FOR HAPPY MEASURES.

This rule is my mantra:
Today is all about you!
There's no need to hold back.
Let your happiness shine through.
So . . .

WooO
Woof
WooF

Shake and shout and shimmy.

Hop and roll and skip.

Twirl and tap and tango.

Leap and bounce and flip!

Commit this next rule to memory.
(Don't worry, there's no test.)
Just remember: On your birthday,
You should try to look your best.

Rule # 3:
Get ready.
Get set.
Get picture
perfect!

But don't get too hung up on the latest birthday style.
The only thing required is a great **BIG** birthday smile.

Rule #4: Do the Math.

Friends
+
Family
=
FUN!

Now that you look the part,
There are two things you should add.
I'm talking about friends and family.
Trust me, you'll be glad.

ding-dong

KNOCK-
KNOCK

DING-
DONG

So gather up your loved ones.
Make sure to-dos have been done.
Then get prepared for one more thing . . .

It's time to have some fun!

In honor of the occasion, here's my birthday decree:
I officially command you to party like you're me!

Percy Isaac Gifford's Birthday Decree

- Put on your party hat.
- Dust off your birthday grin.
- Beat the birthday drums.
- Let the games begin!
- Pin the tail on the donkey.
- Drink the birthday punch.
- Gobble up birthday goodies.
- Laugh a whole, whole bunch.
- Frolic in confetti.
- Revel in the fun.
- Enjoy this piece of good news:
  The party has just begun!

We're coming to my favorite part.
Here's something you should know:

**Anything is good that comes
wrapped up in a bow!**

RULE #6:
THERE'S NO TIME LIKE
THE PRESENT FOR
A PRESENT.

Have fun opening your gifts.
And remember when you're through:
Say "**thank you**" for each one.
That's what good hosts always do.

But wait . . .
A party isn't a party until you hear everyone sing.
Year after year, the birthday song has a happy ring.

RULE #7:
IT AIN'T OVER TILL THERE'S SINGING.

So savor every second.
(It's not a lengthy song!)
Just smile from ear to ear,
Or better yet . . . sing along!

Now, let's talk tradition.
It's important to get this right.
When it's time for birthday cake . . .

rule #8
part A:
have your
cake

Eat every single bite!

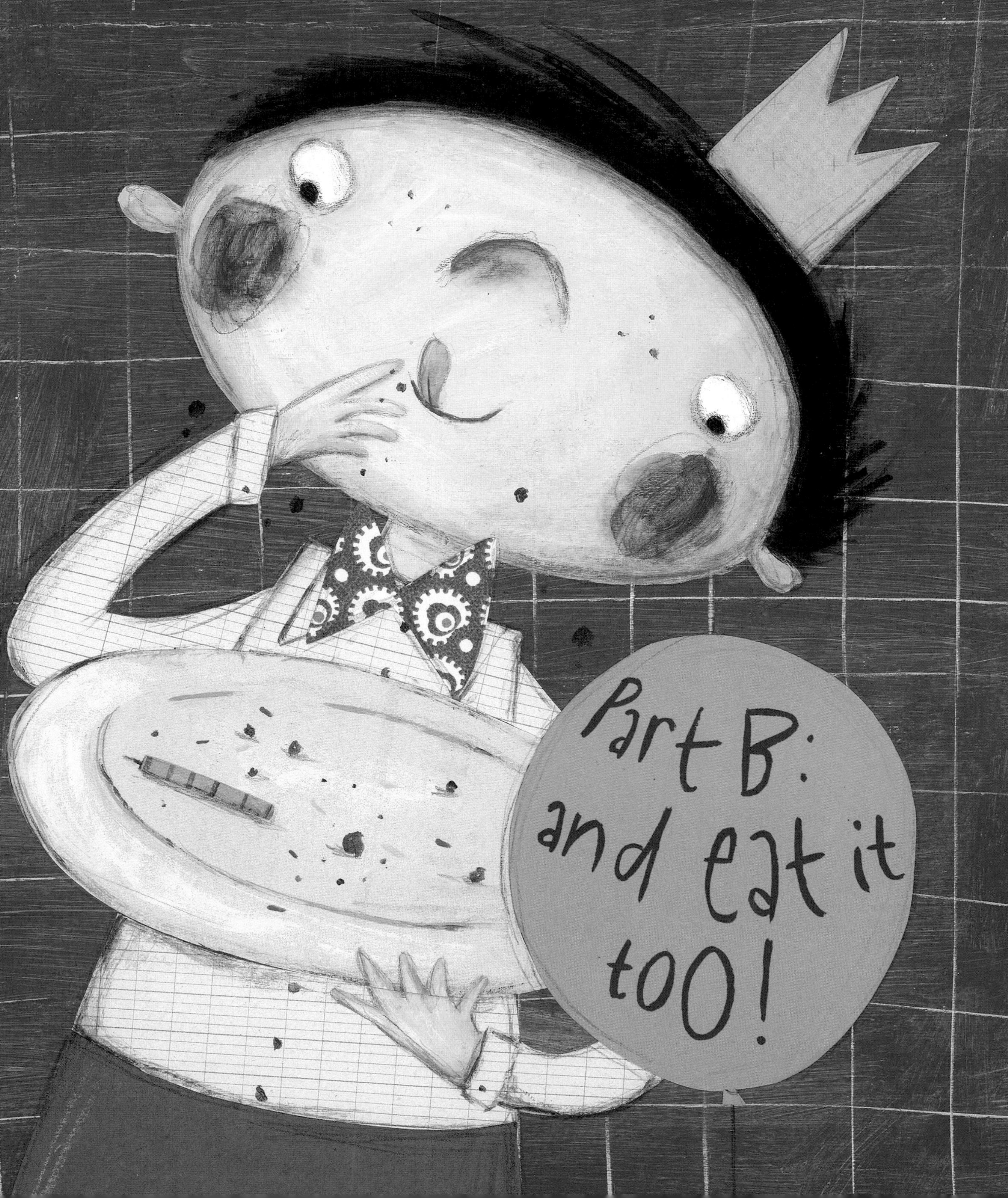

Something else worth noting:
BIRTHDAY WISHES DO COME TRUE!
So make your wish with care.
That's what I always do.

RULE # 9:
BE CAREFUL WHAT
YOU WISH FOR.

Percy's Birthday Wish #1:
Me in a race car.

Alas, we're coming to the end.
Once you've said good-byes,
There's one last thing to consider.
Something **I** always advise.

As you put your gifts away,
And help tidy up and clean,
Take a moment to ask yourself,

What does **all** this mean?

Don't worry. I've got the answer,
though it sounds a bit prophetic:
Growing older is a wondrous thing.
The possibilities are poetic.

GROWING OLDER
A poem by Percy Isaac Gifford

There are many things to try and do,
As you grow, the world's a stage.
It expands with every passing year—
One of the benefits of old age.
(Note: I know you're not all that old,
but age rhymes with stage.)
Your birthday is a starting point.
A whole new year, a whole new you.
Discover life's possibilities!
Have fun, try something new.

So, happy birthday to you, my friend.
As my gift, here's one last rule.
On your birthday, just remember . . .

Growing up is cool!

RULE #10:
BIRTHDAYS
ROCK!